To thank you all
for teaching my children

First published in Great Britain in 1990
by Methuen Childrens Books
A division of the Octopus Publishing Group,
Michelin House, 81 Fulham Road, London SW3 6RB
Text and illustrations copyright © 1990 by Heather S. Buchanan

This edition published 1990 by
Guild Publishing
by arrangement with Methuen Children's Books

Printed in Belgium by Proost International Book Production
CN 8543

George and Matilda Mouse
–and the–
Floating School

Heather S. Buchanan

GUILD PUBLISHING
LONDON · NEW YORK · SYDNEY · TORONTO

There was once a magnificent Dolls' House. It was tucked away in a dark corner of an old town garden.

Inside lived a family of seven mice – George and Matilda Mouse and their five children, Parsley, Mallow, Periwinkle, Columbine and Polyanthus. They were a cheerful, busy family who worked and played by night and slept by day.

The little mice were often very noisy, but inside the Dolls' House, with its glass windows and tin door they were safe from the cat, even when it could hear them squeaking.

But Matilda Mouse was worried. She wanted her children to play with other little mice. More than anything, she wanted them to go to school. She played Blind Man's Buff and Tig with them whenever she could and tried to teach them to read, but it was not the same as being in a proper school.

Suddenly Matilda knew what she must do. She would start her own school!

But a school needed pupils. A very old mouse, called Fergus, who lived nearby in a gardener's boot, had once told George and Matilda about the Rockery Mice. They lived under the rocks by a pond in the middle of the garden.

That night George and Matilda left their children with Fergus and set out to find the Rockery Mice.

Inside the mouse house a ladder of twigs led down into a light and wonderful burrow. There Matilda invited the little Rockery mice to come and learn their lessons with her own children in her new Dolls' House School.

The Rockery Mice were kind and clever garden mice. They already knew all the names and uses of plants in the garden. But they quickly agreed that school would be an excellent idea for their little mice. Lobelia, a grandmother mouse, promised to bring the first pupils the very next night.

The moon was shining brightly as Lobelia and a long line of little mice set out across the slippery rocks beside the pond, on the journey to school. All went well until Dandelion took an unwise leap over two rocks at once and fell, paws over tail, into the pond.

He splashed and squeaked frantically, terrified of the goldfish who lurked in the weeds. Then Lobelia lowered Lavender on her walking stick and she reached out and grabbed Dandelion just before the goldfish got him. Back on the rock Lobelia hugged him better and wrapped him warmly in her shawl.

It was a bedraggled little group that eventually knocked on the Dolls' House door.

Matilda began lessons in the nursery. She used the dolls' counting frame to teach sums. But the Rockery Mice were much more interested in the dolls' toys. Soon these were all over the floor.

Matilda decided to try cookery instead. She took the little mice down to the kitchen where George was in charge of lessons. But he couldn't find enough pots and pans for each mouse so he started an art lesson.

The little mice loved it. They did bubble painting and paw printing using berry jam. When Matilda returned she found George looking very hot and bothered and all the mice covered in jam.

George also taught the little mice to read, using scraps of paper that he collected from the dustbins. Soon they knew all the words on the labels of baked beans tins, crisps packets and sweet wrappers.

They learned their letters from newspaper that had been wrapped round fish and chips.

Matilda was now happy again and pleased with her school. But George thought the mice should learn more about the plants, flowers and insects outside. Helped by the older mice, he built a twig shelter beside the Dolls' House where they could have nature study lessons.

When ladybirds came in, the mice did sums by counting their spots. But when the ladybirds got hungry they would wander off to find new leaves to eat and then the sums were all wrong!

Sometimes a group of friendly worms appeared and curved themselves into letter shapes so the mice could practise their writing.

And once a spider showed them how to weave a web but when the little mice tried to copy it with cotton thread they got terribly tangled up.

During lessons in the shelter, the mice were always very quiet, in case the cat should hear them. But one day Bramble got up during a nature lesson and sang a song he had made up about a bee. It was such a lovely song that Matilda didn't like to stop him but as his little voice rose higher and higher, what she had always dreaded happened. With a crash and a growl the cat was among them!

The terrified mice scurried away in all directions but poor Bramble was caught! Matilda and Fergus hid nearby, staring in horror.

George grabbed a stick. 'Pull Bramble away at the first chance,' he whispered to Matilda.

She nodded, trembling. 'Oh, do be careful,' she squeaked.

George puffed up his chest and strode out in front of the cat, brandishing his stick and squeaking loudly. It had the right effect. The cat's eyes turned on him. With a snarl she sprang forward, releasing Bramble.

As George danced and dived about in front of the furious cat, Matilda crept out of her hiding place. Then George hit the cat's whiskers with his stick. Spitting and yowling, the cat pounced.

Matilda rushed forward and dragged Bramble away.

But George had tripped and dropped his stick. The cat's claw caught his stripey suit and flicked him in the air. George caught a glimpse of snapping yellow teeth as he fell, bruised and exhausted, into a bush.

He couldn't hear the cat now, but he knew she was still crouched in the bushes, waiting for him. Out of the corner of his eye, he saw a familiar sight – the dustbin! Gathering all his strength, George made a dash for it, but the cat was already there!

Now she fancied a game. She chased poor George round and round the dustbin. Then, for fun, she jumped up on top of it to dive down on him. But the dustbin lid wasn't fixed on tightly. As the cat sprang up, it tipped and the whole bin crashed down. The noise brought the cat's owner to the kitchen door and she was told crossly to go inside.

George lay, safe, but shaking with fright under the dustbin lid. His body was aching with pain from his bruises.

But even as he lay there, a smile spread slowly across his battered face, for out of the dustbin had tumbled something truly wonderful!

When George felt stronger, he made his way cautiously back
along the flower bed to the Dolls' House. Long before he got
there, however, he heard familiar squeaks and through the ivy
rushed his anxious family.

They greeted him with tears of joy and relief. Matilda hugged
George and then led him to see poor Bramble, who had now
recovered a little from his terrible experience. He was in the
nursery, sipping tea while Lobelia fussed round, bandaging
his cuts.

For Matilda the nightmare was not yet over. When she was alone again with George there was a knock at the door. Outside was a small group of the older Rockery Mice. News of the disaster had reached their parents and the little mice had been forbidden to return to school. The journey would be too dangerous now the cat knew what they were doing.

Matilda wept. The school would have to close.

To Matilda's surprise, George said nothing. He just smiled mysteriously, handed some strong rope to the Rockery Mice, and told them all to follow him.

When they got to the dustbin, George pushed aside some apple peelings, lifted up a paper bag and stood back proudly to show Matilda his find.

'It's a new school,' he announced happily. 'A floating school!'

At dawn the mice worked hard to drag the toy Noah's Ark to the pond and anchor it securely. They set to, to make paddles and seats for the inside.

They painted pictures for the walls and packed food into the cupboards. There was a peg for each little mouse to hang up its life jacket, and lockers for their pens and paper.

When the floating school was ready, the proud mice rowed it across the pond to show their parents and collect the pupils for the first lessons aboard the Ark.

For George and Matilda it was a dream come true. Now the mice could add pond life to their list of things to study and Fergus promised to start swimming lessons.

But best of all, the cat never interrupted them again, because, of course, cats hate getting their paws wet!